THE PHILLY
FAKE

BALLPARK Mysteries 9

THE PHILLY
FAKE

by David A. Kelly

illustrated by Mark Meyers

A STEPPING STONE BOOK™
Random House 🏠 New York

This book is dedicated to Mark Meyers, who's done an incredible job of bringing Mike, Kate, and the Ballpark Mysteries to life through his illustrations.
—D.A.K.

For the O'Neals with love
—M.M.

"I'm not the manager because I'm always right, but I'm always right because I'm the manager."
—Gene Mauch, Manager, Philadelphia Phillies, 1960–1968

Text copyright © 2014 by David A. Kelly
Cover art and interior illustrations copyright © 2014 by Mark Meyers

All rights reserved. Published in the United States by Random House Children's Books, a division of Random House LLC, a Penguin Random House Company, New York.

Random House and the colophon are registered trademarks and A Stepping Stone Book and the colophon are trademarks of Random House LLC. Ballpark Mysteries® is a registered trademark of Upside Research, Inc.

Visit us on the Web!
SteppingStonesBooks.com
randomhouse.com/kids

Educators and librarians, for a variety of teaching tools, visit us at
RHTeachersLibrarians.com

Library of Congress Cataloging-in-Publication Data
Kelly, David A. (David Andrew)
The Philly fake / by David A. Kelly ; illustrated by Mark Meyers.
pages   cm. — (Ballpark mysteries ; 9)
"A Stepping Stone book."
Summary: Cousins Mike and Kate must help the Philadelphia Phillies' mascot, the Phillie Phanatic, clear his name after the team's bats begin to suspiciously break during games.
ISBN 978-0-307-97785-4 (pbk.) — ISBN 978-0-307-97786-1 (lib. bdg.) —
ISBN 978-0-307-97787-8 (ebook)
[1. Baseball—Fiction. 2. Philadelphia Phillies (Baseball team)—Fiction. 3. Mascots—Fiction. 4. Cousins—Fiction. 5. Philadelphia (Pa.)—Fiction. 6. Mystery and detective stories.] I. Meyers, Mark, illustrator. II. Title.
PZ7.K2936Ph 2014 [Fic]—dc23 2013024343

Printed in the United States of America
10 9 8 7 6 5 4 3 2 1

Random House Children's Books supports the First Amendment
and celebrates the right to read.

Contents

The Crack of the Bat

THWOOMP! THWOOMP! Two hot dogs wrapped in silver foil shot into the air.

"Quick, catch 'em!" Kate Hopkins called to her cousin Mike Walsh. They were on the walkway overlooking the Philadelphia Phillies' baseball field.

But the hot dog missiles soared far to the right. They dropped straight into the hands of fans in the outfield seats.

"Drat!" Mike said. "That wasn't even close!"

"Don't worry," Kate said. "He'll be back."

The Phillies' big green mascot, the Phillie Phanatic, was zipping across the field on the back of an ATV. He wore a red and white Phillies jersey with a star on the back instead of a number. Mounted in front of him was a cannon shaped like a huge hot dog. As the Phillie Phanatic zoomed by the third-base line, he aimed the hot dog launcher at the crowd. *THWOOMP! THWOOMP!* More hot dogs shot into the upper deck.

Mike and Kate were visiting Philadelphia for a big Fourth of July weekend series between the Phillies and the Mets. Kate's mom was a sports reporter, and she often took Kate and Mike with her when she traveled for work. Her friend Carol, who worked for the Phillies, had gotten them tickets for all three games.

The Phillie Phanatic's ATV circled around first base. "Try waving your flags," Carol told them. "Maybe that will get his attention."

With the Fourth of July just two days away, the Phillies had given small American flags to all the fans at the ballpark. Mike and Kate waved their flags high in the air.

"Over here! Over here!" they yelled. Finally, the Phanatic drove Mike and Kate's way.

"This is it," Mike said. He handed his flag to Kate's mom and got ready.

The Phanatic stopped. He aimed his hot dog launcher right at Mike and Kate. He pulled the trigger twice.

THWOOMP! THWOOMP!

Two foil-wrapped hot dogs flew straight for Kate and Mike. They stretched up on their toes to grab them, but the hot dogs sailed right over their heads!

Behind them, two fans caught the hot dogs. They ripped off the foil and took huge bites.

Meanwhile, the Phanatic's ATV zipped off the field as the players returned. The seventh inning was just about to start. The game was tied.

"Sorry, guys," Carol said. "Let's head back to our seats for the rest of the game. The Phillies only have three innings to break this tie!"

Before they had gone very far, Kate tugged Mike's T-shirt. She pointed to a man in a colonial costume near one of the food stands. A small group of fans crowded around him.

"Look," she said. "It's Benjamin Franklin!"

Mike's eyes grew wide. "Really?" he asked. "Maybe he could give me some pointers for my history class!"

"It's not the *real* Ben Franklin, goofball," Kate said. "He'd be over three hundred years old. That man is an actor."

"I knew that," Mike said, rolling his eyes.

He and Kate wormed their way to the front
of the group just in time to see Ben hold up a
kite and a shiny brass key.

"Does anyone know what I did with these?"
Ben asked the group.

Kate waved her baseball cap. "I know!" she said. "You proved storm clouds have an electrical charge."

"Exactly." Ben Franklin nodded. "I also invented a lightning rod, a stove, and lots of other things. Can you guess one of them?"

"Well, I know you didn't invent baseball!" Mike said.

Ben Franklin smiled. "No, but I did invent bifocal glasses," he said, touching the old-fashioned eyeglasses he wore. "They help me see both far away and close up. Maybe those umpires from yesterday's game could have used a pair!"

The Phillies fans laughed.

"Now, if you'll excuse me," Ben said, "I have to go fly a kite!"

The crowd clapped and drifted away. By the time Mike and Kate made it back to their seats, the game had started up again.

For the next couple of innings, it seemed like the Phillies couldn't catch a break. They didn't get any runs in the seventh. The Mets scored three in the eighth. By the bottom of the ninth, the Phillies needed three runs to tie and send the game into extra innings. The first batter got a single. But the next two batters struck out. One more out, and the Phillies would lose the game.

Poodles McGuire, the Phillies' tough little shortstop, stepped up to the plate. He was famous for making big hits just when the team needed them. Poodles let the first pitch go by.

STRIKE!

"Come on, Poodles!" Kate yelled. She waved her flag wildly. Mike stamped his foot and whistled.

When the second pitch came in, Poodles

swiveled his hips and swung with all his might.

POW!

Mike and Kate jumped to their feet. The ball blasted off the bat. It flew high over the outfield. Home run!

As Poodles rounded the bases, a neon Liberty Bell behind the outfield lit up and swung from side to side. Bright blue stars in the bell flashed on and off. A great gonging sound echoed through the stadium.

"Wow! What's that?" Mike asked.

Carol leaned over to explain to Mike and Kate. "It's a giant Liberty Bell made of neon lights," she said. "When a Phillies player hits a home run, it lights up and looks like it's swinging back and forth!"

Poodles crossed home plate. Now the Phillies were only behind by one run! Nolan Addison, the Phillies right fielder and power

hitter, strode up to the batter's box. The crowd roared. Nolan twisted his cleats in the dirt and waited for the pitch.

The Mets pitcher didn't waste any time. He hurled a fastball. Nolan swung from his heels. The bat struck the baseball with brute force. *CRACK!*

But instead of the ball launching over the fence, Nolan's bat cracked apart. The ball bounced weakly to the pitcher, but pieces of the shattered bat flew everywhere!

"Watch out!" Kate cried. A large piece of the bat was coming right at them!

Broken Bats

Everyone ducked and covered their heads.

SPROING!

The chunk of Nolan's bat hit the foul-ball net in front of them.

Kate sat up first. "Saved by the net!" she said.

"We're safe, but the batter wasn't," Carol said. "Nolan was thrown out at first. The Phillies lost because of the broken bat!"

"That stinks! Can't they redo it?" Kate said.

"Nope," Mike said. "The rules say you have to keep playing when a bat breaks. A lot of times the batter gets thrown out because the ball doesn't go very far."

As the fans around them began to file out of their seats, Carol stood up. "Well, it's too bad the Phillies lost," she said. "But how would you like to meet the Phanatic?"

Kate's and Mike's eyes lit up. "That'd be great!" Mike said. "Maybe we can take his ATV for a ride!"

Mrs. Hopkins laughed. "I don't know if *that's* such a good idea," she said. "But you can ask. Don't forget your programs."

Mike and Kate picked up the two baseball programs they had bought before the game. Each had a big picture of the Phillie Phanatic on the cover. They made their way with Mrs. Hopkins and Carol through the stadium to a wide hallway below the stands. The area bustled with stadium workers. A short, squat man with a bushy beard nodded at Carol.

"That's the fifth game we've lost because of a shattered bat!" he said. "My grounds crew is beginning to wonder if it's the Phanatic's fault. You never know what type of joke he's going to play next!"

"I doubt the Phanatic had anything to do with the broken bats," Carol said. "But thanks for the tip, John."

John grabbed a long rake and headed out a tunnel to the field. Carol turned back to Mike, Kate, and Mrs. Hopkins. "That's John, the head groundskeeper," she said. "Don't mind him. He's a bit jealous of all the attention the Phanatic gets."

Just then, Carol's phone buzzed. She checked the screen. "I have to run up to the main office," she said. "The Phanatic should be back any time now. Wait here. He wants to say hi to you."

Ten minutes after Carol left, Mike heard a beeping noise. The Phanatic drove up the hallway on a smaller ATV than the one he had used to shoot hot dogs. He pulled to a stop in front of Mike and Kate and gave them a big wave. When he saw their baseball programs, he grabbed a black marker in his right hand and reached for Mike's program.

"I think he wants to sign it," Mrs. Hopkins said.

Mike held out his program. The Phanatic took it in his left hand and scrawled a big *Phillie Phanatic* across the front. He did the same for Kate. Then he nodded at the back of his ATV.

"You want us to climb on?" Kate asked. The Phanatic gave her a thumbs-up. Kate looked at Mike with a huge smile.

"Can we, Mom?" she asked. "We'll hold on tight!"

"Sure," Mrs. Hopkins said. "But if he asks you to drive, the answer is no!"

Mike and Kate climbed on the small rack on the back of the Phanatic's ATV. There was just enough room for them both to sit down. Their legs dangled over the edge.

The Phanatic's ATV zoomed off down the hallway. *BEEP! BEEP!* The Phanatic tooted the horn as they passed stadium workers cleaning up after the game.

Mike and Kate held on tight. Their feet hung just above the concrete floor. It felt like they were going a million miles an hour.

"Woo-hoo!" Mike cried. "I guess this is what it would feel like if our car didn't have doors."

At the far end, the Phanatic turned around, and they sped back. Kate's brown ponytail trailed out behind her. Her smile was as

wide as the hallway. When they reached Mrs.
Hopkins, Mike and Kate hopped off and gave
the Phanatic a high five.

"That was *so* cool!" Mike said.

The Phanatic parked his ATV in front of

a green door. A sign on the door read PHILLIE PHANATIC LOCKER ROOM. The Phanatic held up a finger, asking them to wait. Then he went inside and shut the door.

"I guess he doesn't like to talk," Kate said.

"But if he did, I'll bet his voice WOULD . . . SOUND . . . LIKE . . . THIS," Mike said in a deep monster voice.

The door opened again, and a man with brown curly hair popped his head out of the room.

"Hello there. Thanks for waiting. I'm Phil," he said as he shook their hands. "I help the Phanatic out with everything he does."

Kate winked at Mike. "We understand," she said. "Maybe you can tell him we said thanks for the ride!"

Phil smiled. "Sure, but I think he already knows," he said. "Would you like to see his locker room?"

"Yes!" Mike and Kate said together.

Phil stepped back and pulled the door all the way open. Mrs. Hopkins, Kate, and Mike went in. Another door in the back wall had a sign on it that read PRIVATE. Pictures of the Phillie Phanatic posing with famous people covered the wall to the right.

Mike pointed at a big picture in the middle of the wall. "Wow, there's the president!" he said. The Phanatic held a giant marker in his right hand and was signing an autograph.

"And there's Merri Monroe, the Olympic gymnast," Kate said, pointing at the next photo. It showed a young woman standing on her hands next to the Phanatic. He was signing the bottom of her shoes.

After looking at the pictures, Mike, Kate, and Mrs. Hopkins took in the rest of the room. In one corner were a chair, a desk, and a big couch. A second desk stood against the left wall. The man sitting at it swiveled around in his chair.

"Hey, you're Ben Franklin!" Mike said. "We saw you earlier with your kite."

Ben laughed. "That's me," he said. He waved his old-fashioned three-cornered hat at them. "It's a pleasure to see you again."

"Ben shares the Phillie Phanatic's locker room," Phil said. "He comes to a lot of the Phillies' home games, but you'll also see him at historic sites around the city. People love to have their picture taken with him!"

"That's right. This weekend I'll be at the tall ships festival at the river, on a ship called the *Eagle*," Ben said. "You should stop by Penn's Landing for the colonial costume contest on Saturday. The winner gets to throw out the first pitch for the Phillies' big game on the Fourth of July!"

"Really?" Mike said. "I'd love to throw out the first pitch!"

"Maybe I could be Betsy Ross," Kate said. "We're going to see her house tomorrow."

"Good idea," Mrs. Hopkins said. "We can look for costumes after we visit the *real* Liberty Bell."

Just then, Carol stepped into the room, clutching a couple of sheets of paper.

"Sorry to interrupt," she said. "But you have to take a look at this."

Carol handed Phil a letter. He let out a low

whistle as he read it, and then dropped it on his desk. They all gathered around to read the note.

Someone had cut out letters of all shapes and sizes from magazines and newspapers and glued them onto the page.

"Oh no!" Kate gasped as she read the words.

GET RID OF THE PHILLIE PHANATIC'S
FRIEND PHIL. HE'S THE ONE MAKING
THE BATS BREAK!

The Liberty Bell

"I haven't done anything to the Phillies' bats," Phil protested. He pointed to the letter. "You know it isn't true. Someone's out to get me!"

Carol stood near the door with her arms crossed. "That's what I thought at first," she said. "I didn't believe you'd tamper with the bats."

"Maybe the Phillies' security people can find out where the letter came from," Mrs. Hopkins said.

"I had them check it over last week," Carol said. "They didn't find any clues."

"You've had the letter for a week?" Phil asked. "Why didn't you tell me?"

"I figured someone was playing a joke on you," Carol said. "After security checked the letter, I thought we'd be able to forget about it. That's why I didn't mention it. But we just got another one, and I'm beginning to wonder."

Carol held out her other hand. In it was a second piece of paper. "Someone slipped *this* note under my office door during tonight's game," she said.

The note looked just like the first one, with all different types of letters.

STILL DON'T BELIEVE ME THAT PHIL'S YOUR PROBLEM? CHECK PHIL'S DESK. IT'S THE BREAK IN THE CASE YOU WERE HOPING FOR!

Phil's eyes grew wide. "What does *that* mean?" he asked.

Carol crossed the room to Phil's desk. "Can you open the drawers, Phil?"

"I don't believe this," Phil said. "Someone's really out to get me." He pulled one drawer open after another. But they only held Phillie Phanatic stickers and pictures. After the last drawer, he shrugged. "See, nothing there."

"Then we need to check under the desk," Carol said. "Kate and Mike, can you look?"

Kate and Mike dropped to their knees. As Mike peeked under the desk, he sucked in his breath. "Oh boy," he said.

Kate scrambled forward and swept her arm under the desk.

Pieces of a shattered baseball bat rolled into the middle of the room!

Ben Franklin let out a loud gasp.

Carol picked up one of the pieces. "I don't think you're breaking the bats, Phil," she said.

"But this is really strange. I am going to have to show this to the team's owner and have security check it out."

Phil shrugged. "I have no idea how that got there," he said, shaking his head.

"*I* believe you, Phil," Carol said. "But I'm not sure the Phillies' owner will. He's pretty upset about losing so many games. Unless we can figure out what's making the bats break, he might bench you for the rest of the season."

The next morning, Mike, Kate, and Mrs. Hopkins toured Philadelphia's historic area. They had just stepped out of Betsy Ross's house when Mrs. Hopkins answered a call on her phone. Mike and Kate waited in a couple of chairs in the courtyard. Mike read through a small book he had bought about the flag.

"Hey, Kate, check this out," Mike said. "Is

it ever okay to fly the American flag upside down?"

Kate studied the small red, white, and blue flags hung around the Betsy Ross house. "No," she said. "Not that I can think of."

"Wrong!" Mike said, handing her the open book. "In an emergency you can fly the flag upside down. It means *send help*."

Kate flipped the page. "Okay, well, if you're so smart, answer this," she said. "What does Alvin 'Shipwreck' Kelly have to do with flags? He was famous back in the 1920s."

Mike shrugged. "I don't know," he said. "Maybe he flew one upside down when he was shipwrecked!"

"Nope!" Kate said. "He set a world record for flagpole sitting! Once he sat on a little platform on top of a flagpole in Atlantic City for forty-nine days and one hour!"

"Wow," Mike said. "And I thought it was hard to sit through math class!"

Kate's mom returned. "That was Carol," she said, putting her phone away. "The security team checked the pieces of the bat under Phil's desk but couldn't find out who broke it."

"That's good," Mike said as they walked toward Independence Hall.

"What do you mean?" Kate asked. "Wouldn't it be better if they could figure out who's breaking the bats?"

"It would," Mike said. "But at least they can't prove it's Phil."

Kate groaned. "Come on! *You* don't think it's Phil's fault, do you?" she asked. "He seemed pretty honest to me."

"Me too," Mrs. Hopkins said. "I hope nothing else goes wrong for him." They crossed the street to Independence Hall. "Carol said if something else happens, they might fire him!"

Independence Hall, a two-story brick building, rose up in front of them. At its center was a tall white tower with a clock. A small group of tourists stood in front of the main entrance. They were gathered around a park ranger wearing a tan shirt, dark green pants, and a wide-brimmed tan hat.

"Here in 1775, the Colonies claimed freedom from England," the ranger said. "Men from each state worked on the Declaration of Independence in this very building. When they were done, they read it to the public in Independence Square. Legend says that they rang the Liberty Bell to celebrate, but historians think that's not really true."

Mike nudged Kate. "I wish I could sign a declaration of independence from homework!" he said.

"Based on your grades, it seems like you already have," Kate said, nudging him back.

The park ranger pointed to a line of visitors near the back of Independence Hall. "You can take tours of the building," he said, "but they're sold out for today. You might want to visit the Liberty Bell instead. It's just across the street."

Kate's mother tapped Mike and Kate on the shoulder. "Well? How does that sound?"

They crossed the street to a long brick-and-glass building. Inside, at the far end, was the Liberty Bell. The big brown bell hung between two posts from a thick piece of wood. A large crack ran from the bottom of the bell almost to the top.

"My teacher said that the crack started tiny," Kate said. "As it grew bigger, they tried to fix it. Then they put bolts at the top and bottom of the crack to hold the sides together."

A park ranger stood next to the bell. "That's right. The Liberty Bell cracked the first time it was rung," he told them. "After it cracked, the city melted the bell down and recast it. Later on, it cracked again. Over time, the bell has

become a symbol of American independence and freedom."

Mike stepped toward a small railing that circled the bell. He didn't need to get close to see the crack.

"Whoa! That crack is like two feet long!" he said.

Kate edged up next to him. "You've cracked enough windows playing baseball," she said. "It's like they picked *you* to ring the bell!"

"I don't know," Mike said. "I'm so strong I probably would have broken it in *half* if I had rung it!"

Kate laughed. Mike always thought he was more powerful than he really was.

As the crowd thinned out, Mrs. Hopkins positioned Mike and Kate in front of the bell for a picture. Then, on their way out, they stopped at the gift shop. Inside were lots of colonial-themed gifts, like bobbleheads of the presidents, copies of the Declaration of Independence, pens made out of feathers, and toy Liberty Bells.

Mike held up a small wooden baseball bat about eight inches long. "Cool! A tiny bat!" he said. Poking out of the handle was the tip of a pen. "And look, I can write with it! Now I can hit a home run in English class!"

At the back of the shop, Kate found a rack of costumes. "Mom! Look! Mike and I could use these for the contest tomorrow!" she called out. She held up George Washington and Betsy Ross costumes.

Mike checked out the George Washington outfit. "Good idea. But I'd want to change it up a little," he said. He put the old-fashioned black hat back on the rack. "I think our George Washington is a Phillies fan. I'll wear a Phillies baseball cap instead of this!"

"Great idea!" Kate said. "And my Betsy Ross could be sewing a Phillies flag!"

Mrs. Hopkins checked the price tags and nodded. "Okay," she said. "Let me pay for the costumes and the pen for Mike and then we'll go back to the stadium for the game. I'll meet you outside."

Mike and Kate walked out into the warm afternoon sun. They were just about to sit down on a bench when they spotted Ben Franklin next to a red brick wall. He was holding his kite and the brass key while a couple of tourists took pictures of him. When the tourists left, Mike and Kate walked over.

"Oh, hello, you two," Ben Franklin said as he put his kite down. "Any news on Phil and the broken bat?"

"Well, my mother heard from Carol this morning," Kate told him. "She said that if anything else goes wrong, they might fire Phil!"

Ben Franklin took off his black three-cornered hat and mopped his brow. Then he glanced over his shoulder and leaned forward.

"Phil's a nice guy," Ben whispered. "But I

have to tell you, he's been acting strange lately. I didn't mention it yesterday because I don't want to get him in trouble."

"What do you mean?" Mike asked.

"Last week when I came into work before a game, I saw Phil leaving the Phillies' dugout," Ben said. "I don't think he'd do anything to the team's bats, but he's not supposed to be in there."

"Maybe *we* could search the dugout for clues," Mike said. "We could wear Phillies shirts and say we're the kids of one of the players."

"I don't think that would work," Ben said. "Players arrange things like that in advance."

"Maybe we could say it's a surprise?" Mike asked.

Ben shrugged. "They're not going to let you in unless you have a good reason," he said.

Kate thought for a moment. She snapped her fingers.

"I've got an idea," she said. "I know how Mike and I can sneak into the dugout before tonight's game to check the bats!"

A Crack in the Case

"Come on, Kate," Mike said. "Can't I have just one?"

"No," Kate said firmly. "We need them to get into the dugout. I saw this on a TV show once, and it worked great."

Mike and Kate were holding big trays of hot dogs covered in relish, mustard, and ketchup. They had used all of Mike's spending money for the weekend to buy them. Kate stepped up to a security guard near the Phillies' dugout. He was standing by a small gate in front of the first row of seats. The gate led onto the field.

"This isn't going to work," Mike whispered to Kate.

"Excuse me," Kate said. "We have a special delivery for the Phillies. We were told to take these to the dugout."

The guard looked down at Kate. Then he glanced over at the Phillies' dugout. A few players were starting to trickle in.

"I'm afraid we're not allowed to let fans on the field before games," the security guard said. "Sorry."

Kate winked at the guard. "We *know* that," she said. "But these are a special birthday surprise for Tim Diamond. All we have to do is go in for a minute and drop them off."

The security guard pushed his baseball cap back and scratched his forehead. "I really don't think I can allow that," he said. "But let me go

check." He walked over to the dugout, talked with a team official, and came back shaking his head.

"I'm very sorry," the security guard said. "But we can't allow anyone in the dugout, even if it is a special occasion. If you want, you can leave the food with me and I'll bring it over."

Kate's smile tightened. "Can't we just drop these off this one time?" she asked him. "Please?"

The security guard crossed his arms. "No, I'm really sorry," he said. "It's against the rules."

Mike shrugged and started up the aisle with his hot dogs. Kate looked once more at the players in the dugout and turned to follow him. But then something farther down the field caught her eye.

"Mike!" Kate said. "Over there!" She nodded at the section to her right and crossed a row of empty seats. Mike followed along.

Kate stopped at the seats in front of right field. A man in a groundskeeper's uniform was tidying up the grass on the other side of the wall.

Kate cleared her throat and held up her tray of hot dogs.

"Excuse me," Kate said when she had his

attention. "We have too many hot dogs. Would you like one?"

A big smile crossed the groundskeeper's face. "Sure," he said. He put his rake down and came over to the infield wall. Kate held out her tray. The man selected one with lots of relish and took a big bite. Mike set his tray down and grabbed a hot dog with just mustard.

"I'm Kate, and this is my cousin Mike," Kate said.

"I'm Louie," the man said between bites. "It's a great night for a game. I just hope nothing goes wrong!"

Kate nudged Mike. "I know!" she said. "What's going on with those broken bats? We've heard it might be one of the Phanatic's jokes."

Louie waved his hand. "Nah," he said after swallowing another bite. "The Phanatic would never do anything to hurt the team."

"How about the Phanatic's friend Phil?" Mike asked. "Someone told us he's been acting strange lately."

Louie shook his head. "I did see something weird last week. I was cleaning up after everyone had gone home when I saw the Phanatic in the dugout. He's usually not around after the games, especially that late."

"What was he doing?" Mike asked.

Louie shrugged. "Hard to tell. I was on the other side of the field," he said. "But he was over in the corner near the locker room stairs. He left after a few minutes."

"Do you think he was doing something to the bats?" Kate asked.

"Nope. He loves the team," Louie said. He finished off the hot dog and licked his fingers. "Anyhow, it's been nice chatting, but I have to get to work. Thanks for the snack!" He ambled back to the patch of grass he'd been working on.

"Wow! Did you hear that? The Phanatic was in the dugout!" Mike said.

Kate scuffed the ground with her sneaker. "I just can't believe it would be Phil *or* the Phanatic," she said. "I wish we could find a way to get into the dugout. I was really hoping the hot dogs would work."

"I still think they were a good idea," Mike said.

"What do you mean?" Kate asked. "They didn't get us into the dugout."

Mike smiled. "I know," he said. "But at least now I won't get hungry during the game!"

After eating a couple of hot dogs each, Mike and Kate gave the rest away to nearby fans and returned to their seats. Carol and Mrs. Hopkins were looking through that day's program.

During the first inning, Mike took out his

new baseball bat pen. Whenever the pitcher threw the ball, Mike pretended to swing at it with his miniature bat. "Another home run for Mike Walsh!" he'd say. Each time he did it, Mrs. Hopkins shook her head and smiled.

Things looked good for the Phillies. Their hot new pitcher, Travis Hunter, struck out three Mets batters in a row. Up at the plate, the Phillies had just as much luck. Their first batter made it to third when the Mets outfielder dropped a long fly ball. The second batter hit a line drive to left field. It fell in for a base hit while the runner on third scored.

Mike punched the air. "All right!" he said. "Now we're up one to zero!"

But the crowd grew silent after the next two Phillies batters struck out. It looked like the Phillies might only get one run for the inning. Then Sammy Masri came up to bat. On his second swing, he hit a towering fly ball to right field.

"Come on! Come on!" Kate called as she jumped to her feet. "It's gotta be a home run!"

Carol and Mrs. Hopkins rose out of their seats and cheered. "Go! Go! Go!" Carol yelled as the ball sailed to deep right.

The Mets right fielder raced back toward the wall. The baseball plunged down, toward the seats. But the Mets player didn't stop. He leapt into the air just as the baseball dropped down over the wall. His glove shot up.

PLOP!

He snagged it! The Mets fielder had caught the ball for the third out!

"Aw, shoot!" Mike said. "I wanted to see the Liberty Bell go off again!"

"I guess we'll have to wait for that," Kate said as they sat down again.

CRUNCH!

A loud cracking sound came from under Mike's right foot. He leaned over and popped back up with his baseball pen.

"Oh no, Mike," Mrs. Hopkins said. "Your new pen!"

"Look, it's fine!" Mike said. "Nothing wrong with it!" He twirled the pen around in his fingers. Then he pretended to bat with it again.

Mrs. Hopkins shook her head and went back to talking with Carol. They were planning a visit to the tall ships event the next day.

"That was a pretty loud crunch!" Kate said to Mike doubtfully.

Mike handed the pen to Kate. It looked fine. But when she tried writing with it on the back of her ticket, a split opened up at the thin end of the pen. It was broken! Kate picked the pen up off the paper. The split disappeared. It looked

normal. She tried writing again. The split
opened up.

Mike's shoulders slumped. "Nuts!" he said.
"I liked that pen."

Kate handed the pen back to Mike. "Sorry," she said. "But at least you've got two things to remember Philadelphia by."

"What do you mean?" Mike asked.

"You've got the pen," Kate said. "And now you've got the crack, too! Just like the one in the Liberty Bell!" She studied the big neon bell in the outfield. Then her eyes lit up. "A crack! That's it, cuz. Give me your pen again!"

Mike handed the pen to Kate.

Kate rolled the miniature bat in her fingers. It looked perfect. But when she pushed on the end of it, the split opened up along the handle.

Kate pointed to the small crack in the bat. "Hey, Mike, look at that! A crack," she said. "I'll bet someone's putting tiny cracks in the Phillies' bats!"

A Perfect Match

"What do you mean?" Mike asked.

Kate pointed to the crack in the Liberty Bell. "What if someone's been putting thin cracks in the bats so that when the players hit a ball, the bat breaks apart? The tiny cracks would be hard to see, but over time the bats would end up breaking! It would be like the Liberty Bell. A tiny crack that grows into a big one!"

"Wow, that might be it!" Mike said. "I wish there was a way to get into the dugout to check the bats."

"There's always a way," Kate said. She twirled the end of her ponytail around her finger. "Maybe you can pretend to be a batboy? Or we could hide in the bathrooms until after the stadium is closed and—"

"Or we could ask Carol if she can bring us to the dugout after the game to take pictures," Mike said. "She'd be able to get us in!"

Kate laughed. "I can't believe I didn't think of that!"

During the next break in the action, Kate asked Carol if they could visit the dugout after the game. Carol thought it was a great idea.

Unfortunately, things didn't line up so well for the Phillies. Even with a home run in the eighth inning, the Phillies couldn't catch up. The Mets won, 3–2.

After the crowd thinned out, Carol led Mike, Kate, and Mrs. Hopkins to a gate in the infield wall. She whispered to the security guard on the other side of the gate. He checked her employee ID and let them onto the field.

The red clay crunched under their feet. "This is great!" Mike said.

Carol scuffed her foot in the dirt. "We're allowed to walk on the warning track," she said. "But stay away from the infield grass. Our head groundskeeper, John, tries to keep visitors off it, since he works so hard to keep it perfect."

Kate checked out the field. The grounds crew was hustling around with rakes and other tools, getting the infield ready for the next day's game. As they reached the dugout, Mike almost bumped into the groundskeepers' green cart that was parked in front of it.

Mike and Kate bounded down the dug-out steps. The dugout was empty except for paper cups on the floor and some towels on the benches. In the corner were bins full of dozens of bats. Mike and Kate wanted to head right for the bats, but Carol made them sit with Mrs. Hopkins on the long bench against the back wall while she took pictures. Mike kept messing up the pictures because he was fidgeting so much.

"It's hard to sit still with the bats so close!" he whispered to Kate.

"One more picture!" Carol said. "This time with the Phillies logo in the background."

Finally, Carol was done.

"Now's the time," Kate whispered to Mike.

They walked to the corner of the dugout, near the stairs down to the locker room. The bins filled with bats sat under shelves of batting helmets.

"So what are we looking for, Sherlock?" Mike asked.

"I'm not sure. A crack maybe," Kate said. "Or anything that doesn't seem right."

They pulled up one bat after another. There were brown bats and black bats and new bats and old bats. But none seemed to have any cracks.

Mike held up a tan bat. He was about to put it back when something caught his eye. "Kate, look," he said.

"What?" Kate asked. "I don't see any cracks."

Mike pointed to a line of red dust across the middle of the bat. "Take a closer look," he said.

Kate leaned in. The red dust on the bat handle had marks in it! Zigzag lines ran through it.

"I'll bet it's like my bat pen," Mike said.

Mike took the bat and placed the end of its handle on the dugout floor. He held the bat at an angle and pushed.

Nothing happened.

Then he turned the bat a little and did it again.

This time, a split appeared in the handle, just above the red dust marks! Mike searched the bins for another bat with red dust marks. When he found one, he tested it the same way. It had a split, too!

"See?" Mike said. "Someone *is* putting cracks in the bats!"

"But how?" Kate asked. "They're too thick to step on like your baseball pen."

Mike pointed to the zigzag pattern in the red dust. "But they're not too thick to drive over," he said. "Those are tire marks!"

Mike and Kate riffled through the rest of the bats in the bin. Now that they knew what they were looking for, the damaged bats were easy to spot. By the time they went through all of them, Mike and Kate had found five bats with tire marks on them. Kate called Carol and her mom over.

Mike held up one of the bats. He pressed its handle on the ground.

Carol and Mrs. Hopkins both gasped when the handle split open.

"Somebody's driving over the bats," Kate

said. "It must crack them just enough inside so they'll break but look normal on the outside."

"How would someone get a car in here to run over the bats?" Carol asked.

Mike traced the zigzag treads with his finger. "It's not a car," he said. "That would leave bigger marks. It's something smaller."

"Like what?" Mrs. Hopkins asked.

Mike looked up at the infield. The groundskeepers in their green shirts were raking the infield dirt, stirring up clouds of red dust. "I think I know," he said.

Mike ran up the dugout stairs with the bat and raced down the warning track to the other end of the dugout. He skidded to a stop in front of the groundskeepers' green cart that they had passed on the way in. When everyone else caught up, Mike knelt down and held the bat next to a tire.

The tread marks didn't match at all!

"Oh rats!" Mike said. "I guess it's not a groundskeeper. I was sure the cart made those marks!"

Kate let out a low whistle.

"Well, I've got another idea," she said. "But

no one's going to like it!"

"Why not?" Mrs. Hopkins asked.

"Don't blame me," Kate said. "But I think we need to check the tires on the Phillie Phanatic's ATV!"

"Oh no!" Carol said.

The four of them hurried through the stadium to the hallway where the Phanatic's ATV was parked.

Mike knelt down again and placed the dusty tread marks on the bat next to the ATV's tire.

Kate gasped.

It was a perfect match!

The Lost Phanatic

"I just can't believe it would be Phil or the Phanatic!" Mike said as they got out of a taxi the next morning. It was ten o'clock, and they had just arrived at Penn's Landing for the tall ships festival. Families, street performers, and kids dressed up in colonial costumes wandered around the open brick plaza.

"Don't worry," Mrs. Hopkins said. "Carol told me they're checking the tire marks on the bats. She'll give us an update at the Phanatic's autograph signing. The only thing you two should be worrying about is the costume contest!"

"No problem," Mike said. "How do I look?"

Mrs. Hopkins stood back to examine him. He was dressed like a cross between a Phillies player and George Washington. He wore tan pants and a ruffled white shirt with a long blue coat like George Washington, but bright red kneesocks like a Phillies player. Instead of an old-fashioned hat, he wore a Phillies baseball cap over a white curly wig. He had a baseball glove on his left hand.

"You look great, Mike," Mrs. Hopkins said.

"I don't know," Mike said. "I still wish I had an ax. It'll be a little hard to chop down that cherry tree with my glove."

Kate grinned and pretended to swing a baseball bat. "The only things you've ever chopped at are all the pitches you've missed!" she said.

Kate's costume was unusual, too. In one hand, she held a Phillies flag. In her other, she had a needle and length of dark blue thread. Kate was dressed as Betsy Ross, with a white cap, a blue shirt, and a bright red, white, and blue skirt that looked like a flag. She also wore baseball socks and red and silver sneakers.

Mike straightened the curly white wig under his Phillies baseball cap. "We've got to win that contest," he said. "I really want to throw out the ball at tonight's game!"

Mrs. Hopkins led them through the crowd to a large building at the end of the plaza. Big letters on the building spelled out SEAPORT MUSEUM. They followed MEET THE PHANATIC signs inside.

Parents and children filled the large room. Many of them had Phillies baseball caps, T-shirts, or programs for the Phanatic to sign. Carol stood near the back wall.

"You two look great!" Carol said to Mike and Kate as they walked over. "I feel like I've stepped back in time to 1776!"

Kate curtsied to Carol. Mike tipped his hat. "Is the Phanatic here?" Kate asked.

Carol shook her head. "Not yet," she said, checking her watch. "Hopefully nothing will go wrong. My boss wants to keep an eye on him until they figure out what's happening to the bats."

After ten minutes, the Phanatic still hadn't shown up. The crowd was restless. Some of the children were running around the room playing tag. Carol kept checking her watch. She was about to make a call when the door opened and everyone looked up.

But it wasn't the Phillie Phanatic.

It was Ben Franklin!

He gazed at the crowd through his bifocal

glasses. Then he held up his hands and gave them a big smile.

"I know you're here to see our city's favorite mascot," Ben said. "But I heard he couldn't make it today, so I thought I'd stop by."

Ben walked to the front of the room as the children sat back down. "Maybe you'd like to hear how I almost got shocked by lightning flying my kite during a storm!" he said. "Or how I helped the United States win the Revolutionary War!"

For the next twenty minutes, Ben kept the audience on the edge of their seats. When he finished, he signed autographs.

"Wow! Ben did a great job!" Carol said. "It's funny. A few years ago he applied for Phil's job, but we picked Phil instead. As much as I like Phil, Ben Franklin is really good!"

"Did you hear that?" Kate whispered to

Mike. "Ben Franklin applied for Phil's job! That's weird."

Carol pulled out her phone. "I've got to find out what happened to the Phanatic," she said as she walked to a quiet spot and called the stadium. When she returned, she looked sick.

"I just talked to John, the head grounds-keeper," Carol said. "He saw Phil at the ball-park early this morning. He said Phil left two hours ago. Something's wrong!"

"What do you think happened?" Mike asked.

"I don't know," Carol said. "But the Phanatic *has* to be at the big Fourth of July show after tonight's game! There's a special event planned. I've got to go back to the stadium to see what I can find out."

As they left the building, Ben Franklin was still signing autographs. Once they were outside, Carol said goodbye and headed for the parking lot.

Kate tugged at her mother's sleeve. "Can Mike and I look around?" she asked.

Mrs. Hopkins nodded. "We have about an hour before the costume contest." She pointed to the tall ship the *Eagle*. "I'll meet you up on deck."

"Okay, great!" Kate said. She gave her mother a hug. "We'll see you in a little while! Can you hold on to some of our stuff until the contest?"

Mrs. Hopkins nodded. Mike handed her his baseball glove. Kate turned over her Phillies flag and the needle and thread. Then she and Mike ran to explore the plaza.

"I hope Phil's okay," Kate said as they headed for a ringtoss booth. "It's weird he didn't show up. Maybe his car broke down."

"He probably would have called Carol if it did," Mike said. "Hopefully he'll turn up before the game tonight."

The line was too long at the ringtoss booth, so Mike and Kate stopped at the American history booth next to it. Kate won a Liberty Bell sticker by answering three questions correctly. Mike got two correct, so he won a USA sticker.

As they turned to leave, Mike spotted a man dressed as a giant lemon. He was yellow from head to toe and was handing out something to people walking by. Mike and Kate ran over. The man handed them a flyer. "It's a coupon good for ten percent off a Philly cheesesteak and lemonade," he said.

"A Philly what?" Kate asked.

"A Philly cheesesteak. It's a sub roll filled with thin slices of steak and melted cheese," the lemon man said. "They're one of Philadelphia's favorite foods."

"Sounds great! Let's get one!" Mike said.

After waiting in line, Mike and Kate ordered two cheesesteaks and lemonades. They found a bench in the shade and sat down to eat.

"Yum," Mike mumbled with his mouth full.

"Me gusta," Kate agreed. "I like it!" She was teaching herself Spanish. Kate wanted to be like her father, who was a scout for the Los

Angeles Dodgers. He spoke Spanish because he worked with a lot of players from Spanish-speaking countries.

As they were throwing their wrappers away, Kate nodded to the other side of the plaza. "Hey, there's the Phillie Phanatic," she said. "He finally made it!"

The Phanatic was standing under a tree on the far side of the plaza. A small crowd had gathered around him as he signed autographs.

Mike and Kate watched the Phanatic for a few minutes from the back of the crowd. They waved, trying to get his attention, but the Phanatic seemed to be ignoring them.

As they watched, Kate frowned. Something didn't seem right, but she couldn't put her finger on what.

Fans from the crowd kept handing the Phanatic things to sign. He'd take them in his right hand, sign them with his left hand, and then give them back. Kate watched him sign six different things the same way.

Kate thought about all the photos she had seen in the Phanatic's locker room. Then it hit her. She clapped her hands over her mouth and gasped.

"Mike!" Kate said. "He's not real!"

Mike looked at her. "Huh? You think the Phanatic is a robot?" he asked. "That would be cool!" Mike stuck his arms straight out and started to talk in a robot voice. "This—does—not—compute."

Kate shook his shoulder until Mike stopped being a robot.

"That's not what I meant," she said. "What I mean is that's not the real Phillie Phanatic! He's a fake!"

Green Clues

"We saw a lot of photographs in the Phanatic's locker room, remember?" Kate asked Mike. "In the photos, he's always signing with his *right* hand. This Phanatic is signing with his *left* hand!"

"I don't know," Mike said. "It sure looks like the Phanatic. If that's not the Phanatic, then who is it?"

Kate crossed her arms and rocked back on her heels. "I'll bet it's Ben Franklin!" she said.

Mike's mouth dropped open. "What?" he asked. "How could it be him?"

"He's trying to get Phil's job!" Kate said. "You heard Carol. Ben Franklin tried out for it. Then he showed up this morning instead of the Phanatic. I'll bet he did that because he knew Carol would be watching. He wanted to show how good he was with kids!"

"He also shares the Phanatic's office, so he could have planted the broken bat that first day," Mike said. "That would mean that Ben Franklin is causing all the trouble. He's trying to get rid of Phil so he can take over his job!"

Kate bit her lip. "I've got an idea," she said.

She moved closer to the Phillie Phanatic. Children crowded around him, getting things signed.

"Hey, Charlie! Hey, Phil! Hey, Jimmy, over here!" Kate called.

Nothing happened.

Kate looked over her shoulder and gave Mike a thumbs-up. She had a plan. She turned back to the Phillie Phanatic.

This time, Kate yelled, "Hey, Ben Franklin, over here!"

The Phillie Phanatic glanced up from the book that he was signing and looked directly at Kate.

Kate waved.

The Phillie Phanatic stopped for a moment. Then he shook his head and returned to signing things for the children.

Kate ran back to Mike.

"That's Ben Franklin, all right!" Kate said.

"Let's find a police officer!" Mike said. He scanned the plaza. "There must be one around here." He was about to take off when Kate stopped him.

"We need more proof," Kate said. "I wish Phil was here! He'd know if that's the real Phanatic!"

"Let's find your mom," Mike said. "Maybe she can call Carol."

"Okay," Kate said. She checked the time. "The costume contest is about to start. Mom should be waiting for us on the *Eagle*."

They ran across the plaza to the ship. Kate bounded up the gangplank. At the top, she turned around. Mike was still near the bottom.

"Mike! Come on!" Kate called. "We've got to find my mom before the contest!"

"Hold up!" Mike called out. "Look at this." He pulled something off the split wood in the handrail. It was a few pieces of green fur!

Kate ran back down the gangplank. Mike showed her the inside edge of the handrail. The fur had been caught on a splinter.

Kate took the strands of green from Mike's fingers. "It looks like the Phillie Phanatic's fur!" she said.

"That's what I thought," Mike said.

Just then, an announcement came over the ship's loudspeaker. *"The costume contest is starting. Please go to the front of the ship to register."*

"Let's come back to this later," Mike said. "I really want to win so I can throw out the first pitch at tonight's game!"

But as they rushed up the gangplank, another piece of green fur caught Kate's eye. "The Phillie Phanatic *must* have come by here," she said. "He's the only one around with green fur like that!"

Mike studied the fur. "You think this is from the fake Phanatic or the real one?" he asked.

"I don't know," Kate said. "But we need to find out."

At the top of the railing, they found a third piece.

"What do we do?" Mike asked.

"We can get to the contest a little late," Kate said. "It will take them a while to get through all the kids."

The gangplank ended at the deck of the ship. To the left were the front of the boat and the costume contest. To the right was the side deck.

Kate turned to the right. "Let's start looking here," she said. "There are too many people up front. We can check the rest of the ship next."

Mike and Kate searched the deck and the side rail, but they found nothing odd. They heard the announcer call the name of the first kid in the costume contest. Mike was just about to give up when he spotted more green fur caught in the doorway.

"Kate! Here's some more!" he said, holding up the strands. "He must have gone through here."

Mike and Kate stepped through the doorway. A few feet inside, Kate found a wisp of green fur caught on a door latch. Just past that, the hallway split. On one side was an open area at the back of the ship. On the other, a flight of stairs led belowdecks. A small chain hung across the stairs. It read EMPLOYEES ONLY.

Mike looked around to make sure no one was watching. Then he undid the chain. "Let's try the stairs," he said.

"We'll just say we were looking for a bathroom if anyone asks," Kate said. After they slipped past, Mike hooked the chain again.

A quick search at the top of the stairs revealed no fur.

Kate nodded to the deck below. They scampered down the narrow stairs. On the bottom step, Kate found a few strands of green fur. "Bingo!" she said.

Ahead of them, the lower deck opened out into a bigger space. White cloth hammocks hung in rows down the middle of the deck. On the other side of the hammocks was a row of doors.

Kate twisted her ponytail around her finger. "If the Phanatic was here, he must have been in one of those rooms," she said.

Without wasting time, they dodged the hanging hammocks and ran to the first door. Kate opened it. A large Philadelphia Phillies duffel bag sat in the corner. Mike unzipped it.

"You'll never believe this," he said. From the bag, Mike pulled out Ben Franklin's head!

Kate screamed.

Mike laughed. "Got you!" he said.

Kate looked closer. In Mike's hands was a plastic dummy's head, wearing Ben Franklin's glasses, his white curly wig, and his three-cornered hat.

Kate stamped her foot. "You scared me!" she said.

Mike dropped the head back in the bag. "It's Ben Franklin's whole costume," he said.

Kate glanced around the room. "He must have changed in here after leaving the Seaport Museum," she said. "Remember? The first day we met him, he said he'd be on the *Eagle*. He put on a fake Phillie Phanatic costume and went out to sign autographs! All that green fur we found was from his costume. It probably snagged on the ship as he left."

"Let's check the rest of the rooms for other clues," Mike said. For the next few minutes, they ran from room to room. Every one was empty. Kate was about to quit when she heard Mike's voice.

"Kate, give me a hand!" he called. He was standing by a heavy wooden door at the very back of the ship. The walls on both sides of the door were made from thick planks of wood. A large iron pin was jammed in the door's handle. Mike was trying to remove it, but his hands kept slipping.

"I can't get this out!" Mike said.

Kate grabbed the top of the pin with Mike. On the count of three, they gave the pin a strong yank.

For a moment, nothing happened.

"Try again!" Mike said. "One, two, three!"

This time, the pin made a sharp metallic squeak when they pulled. It slid away from the handle.

Mike pushed on it, and the door popped open.

Inside was Phil! He was wearing a red Phillies T-shirt and shorts, but beads of sweat stood out on his forehead.

He rushed to the door. "Thanks for finding me!" he said, breathing a big sigh of relief. "I've

been trapped in here for hours! When I find out
who locked me up, they're going to be in *big*
trouble!"

"What happened?" Mike asked.

"Just before the Phanatic was getting ready to come and sign autographs, I got a phone call," Phil explained. "The caller told me to meet him here as soon as possible and he'd tell me who was breaking the bats. But when I got here, the door shut, and I couldn't get out! I tried yelling and pounding, but the walls are too thick. No one could hear me."

Phil ran his fingers through his hair. "I've got to find out who did this!" he said.

"You're in luck," Kate said. "I think we know where to look."

Phil's eyes opened wide. "You do?" he asked. "Where?"

"Out on the plaza," Mike said. "Come on."

Mike, Kate, and Phil ran through the ship and down the gangplank. They hurried through the crowd until they came to the tree on the far side of the plaza. The fake Phillie

Phanatic was still signing autographs, surrounded by a group of kids.

"Hey, that's not the Phillie Phanatic!" Phil said.

"We know," Mike said. "It's Ben Franklin!"

Phil looked around until he spotted a police officer.

"Come on," Phil said. "Let's get help. We've got to stop him before tonight's game!"

A Fabulous Fourth

That night, before the Phillies game, Thomas Jefferson strode up to the pitching mound. At least, a *young* Thomas Jefferson did. The winner of that morning's costume contest went into his windup and hurled the ball toward home plate. It fell short. The ball bounced once in the dirt before the catcher caught it. He ran it back out to Thomas Jefferson, who held it up while the fans cheered.

Mike and Kate watched from their front-row seats near the Phillies' dugout with Mrs.

Hopkins and Carol. "I guess you wish that you were out there throwing that first pitch," Mrs. Hopkins said to Mike.

Mike scuffed at the ground with his sneaker. "Sort of," he said. "*I* would have been able to make it over the plate!"

"But it was worth missing the costume contest to rescue Phil," Kate said. "Even if we didn't get to throw out the first pitch!"

Mike perked up. "Yeah," he said. "At least we get to see the Phillie Phanatic one more time before we go home."

Carol leaned over. "And he told me that he might have something special for you two," she said. "Just wait until after the game."

"Cool!" Mike said.

"Speaking of the Phanatic, what happened to Ben Franklin?" Mrs. Hopkins asked.

Carol shook her head. "After Mike and Kate

rescued Phil, he found a policewoman," she said. "The fake Phanatic really *was* Ben Franklin, just like Kate thought. He had a fake Phanatic costume specially made. Before he was caught, he was planning on being the Phillie Phanatic for tonight's Fourth of July game!"

"Then why did he show up at the Seaport Museum?" Kate asked.

"It's tricky," Carol said. "Ben Franklin wanted to come in and save the day. He was hoping the broken bats would force us to fire Phil and hire him instead."

"So *he* was the one breaking the bats?" Mrs. Hopkins asked.

"Yup. After everyone went home, he drove the Phanatic's ATV over the bats to crack them. The cracks were too small to see, but over time the bats would break," Carol said. "Then he'd dress up as the

Phanatic and put the cracked but normal-looking bats in the dugout."

"He told us that he saw *Phil* in the dugout," Mike said. "He was trying to blame Phil."

"So Ben must have planted the shattered bat under Phil's desk," Kate said. "And then sent those notes to Carol. He really wanted the Phillies to get rid of Phil."

"That's right," Carol said. "Unfortunately for him, the only person we'll be getting rid of is Ben Franklin!"

As the game began, the Phillies jogged out to their positions on the field. After a few warm-up throws from the pitcher, a Mets batter stepped up to the plate. The Phillies were playing the Mets one last time.

Right from the start, the game was exciting. Both teams scored runs in each of the first three innings. First the Mets were ahead. The

Phillies tied it. Then the Mets pulled ahead again, and the Phillies tied it again. Then both teams did the same thing the next inning, which left the score tied.

No one scored in the fourth, fifth, or sixth innings. In the seventh, with the game tied and two men on base, Poodles McGuire walked to the plate. Mike jumped to his feet. "This is it!" he yelled. "Nail it! Come on, Phillies!"

"I sure hope they found all of those bats with tiny cracks," Kate said. "We could really use a home run now."

On the third pitch, Poodles walloped the ball deep to right field. The two men on base started to advance as they watched the ball.

Mike pumped his fist. "Go! Go! Go!" he shouted. All around them, Phillies fans were hollering like crazy.

The ball sailed over the outfield wall. It was

a home run! Behind center field, the giant neon Liberty Bell swung back and forth as the runners headed for home.

Mike and Kate high-fived. The runners crossed home plate one after the other. The Phillies were ahead by three runs.

With two more innings, the Mets couldn't catch up. The Phillies won the game, 6–3!

"Can you believe it?" Carol said. "We won! And no broken bats the whole game! Thanks to you two!"

Kate and Mike blushed.

Carol glanced at right field. "Now's the best part," she said. "Keep your eye on that doorway on the field. I think something special is coming!"

Mike and Kate jumped up to watch. A minute later, the doors opened and the Phillie Phanatic zoomed out on his ATV.

But instead of zipping around the field and joking with the players, the Phanatic drove over to where Kate and Mike were sitting. He stopped right in front of their seats. Then he hopped off his ATV and raised his arms up so the fans would cheer.

The crowd went wild. The Phanatic pulled out a piece of wood with a big red button in the middle from the back of his ATV. All around Mike and Kate, the Phillies fans grew silent. The Phanatic held the button in front of Mike and Kate as if he was expecting them to do something.

Kate glanced at Mike. "I think he wants us to push the button," she said. She put her finger on the button. Mike added his finger.

"Ready?" Mike asked.

Kate nodded.

"On three," Mike said. "One ... two ... three!"

They pushed the button.

Nothing happened.

But after a few seconds, they heard *FOOMP! FOOMP! FOOMP!*

Then they saw three lines of sparks rise up into the night from behind the stadium's outfield wall.

"What's going on?" Mike asked. "What'd we do?"

Before Kate could answer, three giant fireworks explosions lit up the sky! Huge circles of red, white, and blue burst overhead.

"Ooh!" the crowd cried out.

FOOMP! FOOMP! FOOMP! FOOMP!

Four more giant rounds of fireworks exploded over the Phillies' stadium.

"Aah!" went the crowd.

As the brightly colored sparks fell to earth, the Phillie Phanatic gave Mike and Kate high fives. Fireworks lit up the sky for fifteen more minutes.

At the end, Mike and Kate heard dozens of small explosions all at once.

FOOMP! FOOMP! FOOMP! FOOMP! FOOMP! FOOMP! FOOMP! FOOMP!

The sky turned almost as bright as day. A final cluster of red, white, and blue fireworks exploded overhead.

When it was done, the crowd was quiet. Then the stadium burst into applause.

"That was amazing!" Kate said.

"I'll say," Mike said. "This was the best Fourth of July ever!"

Dugout Notes
☆ The Phillies' Ballpark ☆

Phillie Phanatic. According to the Phillie Phanatic's bio, he's six feet six inches tall and weighs 300 pounds. He was born on the Galápagos Islands. Two of his favorite foods are cheesesteaks and soft pretzels!

Liberty Bell replica. To honor the real Liberty Bell just across town, the Phillies have a giant neon version. The Phillies' Liberty Bell is on a tall tower in right-center field. The light is fifty feet tall and thirty-five feet wide. That's about as big as a house! After each Phillies home run, the Liberty Bell lights up bright white with blue stars. There's even a giant neon crack up the front. The bell swings back and forth and rings loudly in celebration.

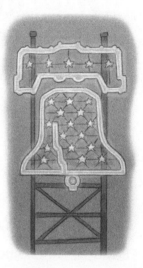

Staying put. The Phillies have been around since 1883! While some teams have moved, the Phillies have always been in Philadelphia. And they've always been called the Phillies.

Hot dog launcher. The Phillie Phanatic really does have a hot dog launcher. It can shoot hot dogs a few hundred feet!

Winning at losing. The Philadelphia Phillies set the record for the team with the most losses. They have over 10,000 losses. But that record isn't as bad as it sounds. They have had about 9,000 wins during the same time. Since they're one of the oldest baseball teams, they've played a lot more games than most other teams. More games mean more losses, even if they're a good team.

Ashburn Alley. On the walkway behind center field is Ashburn Alley. It's named for famous Phillies player Richie Ashburn. Ashburn was a center fielder for the Phillies in the fifties. The alley is filled with food stands and picnic tables, but it's also a place to learn Phillies history. The alley's All-Star Walk shows the Phillies players who have been all-stars. It also has a Wall of Fame for famous Phillies players.

Bi-level bullpens. The Phillies' stadium features two bullpens, where pitchers can warm up. But the Phillies' bullpens are special because one is almost on top of the other. The top one is near Ashburn Alley, so fans can get a close-up view of pitchers. The bottom one is level with the outfield. The visiting team gets the top bullpen, close to the fans. That way, the fans can give the opposing pitchers lots of "advice."

Ben Franklin. There wasn't much that Ben Franklin couldn't do. He was one of

America's Founding Fathers and played an important role in the American Revolution. But he also was a famous author, inventor, and scientist. He created things like lightning rods, bifocal glasses, and medical devices that are still used today. He also founded America's first lending library.

BATTER UP AND CRACK THE CASE!

BASEBALL SLEUTHING FUN
WITH MORE TO COME!

RandomHouseKids.com